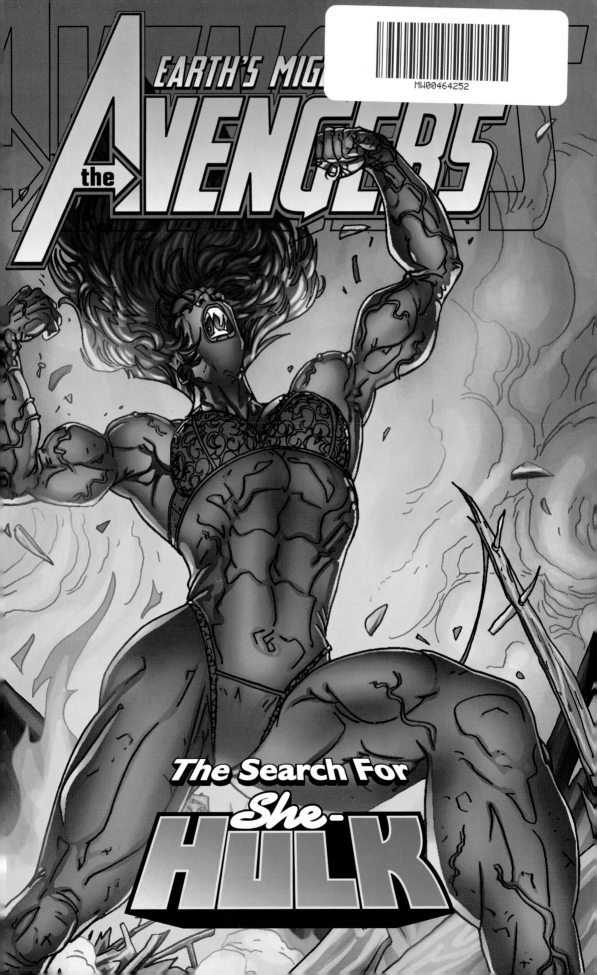

The Search For

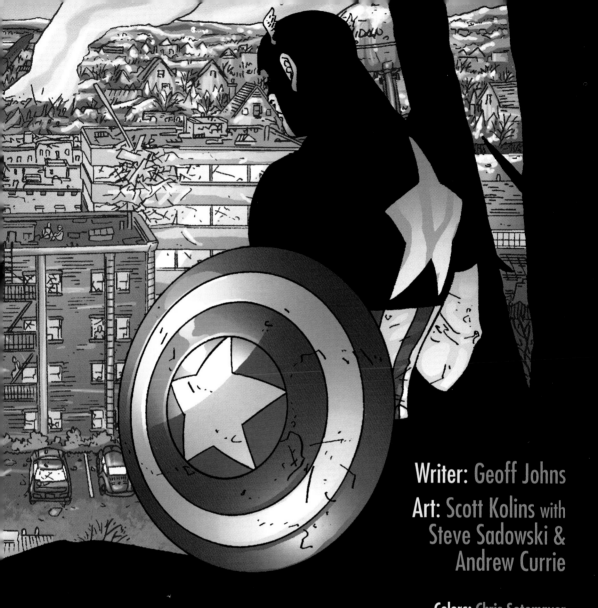

Writer: Geoff Johns
Art: Scott Kolins with
Steve Sadowski &
Andrew Currie

Colors: Chris Sotomayor
Letters: Virtual Calligraphy's Rus Wooton
Cover Art: Jae Lee & Jose Villarrubia
Assistant Editors: Marc Sumerak,
Andy Schmidt & Nicole Wiley
Editor: Tom Brevoort

Collections Editor: Jeff Youngquist
Assistant Editor: Jennifer Grünwald
Book Designer: Meghan Kerns

Editor in Chief: Joe Quesada
Publisher: Dan Buckley

PREVIOUSLY IN AVENGERS...

Trusted by the public, and recognized as a world power unto themselves by the United Nations, they are Earth's Mightiest Heroes, united to protect us from any threat imaginable.

They are THE AVENGERS!

Their leader, Captain America, has made it his mission to instill as much trust amongst the members of the Avengers as the public has in the team itself. With the abundance of alpha personalities involved, and their diverse backgrounds, this is not an easy task.

Recently, She-Hulk's level of gamma radiation was depleted by fellow teammate and human nuclear reactor Jack of Hearts. This transformed her from the fun, intelligent She-Hulk into a Jekyll and Hyde monstrosity, much like her cousin. Now in Human form, Jennifer has run away from the Avengers, seeking help elsewhere...and feeling horribly alone.

LAS VEGAS, NEVADA

--the *Star Trek Experience*. It wasn't actually like *being* in *space*. And that *teleportation*?

Light shows just don't *excite* you much once you've been on a *Kree battleship*.

Or seen the *Collector's* living quarters.

The Collector's *bad breath* is an *experience* all its *own!*

I know *you* were the one that invited *me* here, Jan, but...we're in *Vegas*.

So I've *got* to gamble...

Janet Van Dyne--

Can we just... we're having a *great* time.

But it's going to *end*, isn't it? Something's going to screw this up.

I wasn't a very good husband, was I?

No. You weren't.

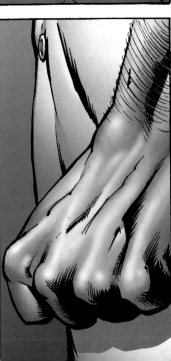

When I first *discovered* the *particles* that enable us to *control* our size, to *shrink* or *expand*--

--I thought I finally *succeeded* in life.

I thought I'd be this great *hero.* Get my face on *Scientific American* or *Time* or something...

But my *ego* wouldn't *let* me *succeed.* God... look at it, Jan. I called those particles..."*Pym Particles.*" I named them after *myself.*

Could that be any *more* ridiculous?

You were *proud.*

No. I was lost in my own little *fantasy* of *self-importance.* And when we first *founded* the *Avengers*...I...

I felt over-shadowed by *Iron Man, Thor* and...even *you.* Why do you think I kept changing identities over the years?

From *Giant-Man* to *Goliath* to *Yellowjacket.*

I was *never* good enough.

What did you do with the *first ring* I gave to you?

You didn't *keep* it, did you?

No. I was *angry*, I wanted to *forget*.

And the money went to a good cause. My father's *scholarship* fund.

He was a brilliant scientist. I'd hate to think what he would say today if he knew what I...

You have every reason to say *no*.

I *know* I do. But it doesn't mean I don't *love* you.

Can you understand that?

No *Avengers* around, Wasp.

...WHIRLWIND?

No one but *you* two.

Dammit.

Your *ex* is taking a *nap.* I'm getting a little *tired* myself.

What do you *want,* Cannon?

VWWSSSTT!

AAARR!

Revenge for *tossing* you in *prison?*

GO AHEAD. TRY AND FLY AWAY, CANNON. I'LL CRUSH YOU LIKE A BUG.

Try...Trying to *intimidate* me? Doesn' matter *how* big you get, Ant-Boy.

Doesn'...

I wasn't put on this *world* for *anyone* but *me.*

I don't owe *you* anything.

You were given a *gift*, Cannon. A mutant ability to become a *human whirlwind*.

You *chose* your *path*.

But you *fail* to take *responsibility* for it.

And *that* is what makes you a *criminal*.

Thor, Iron Man and Captain America?

You *wish* you had it *that* easy.

CHING

You're from out of town, *hm?*

I...I just want some breakfast.

We've got *great* waffles. Old *Bone* recipe.

What will three dollars buy?

No worries. Three dollars will get you *whatever* you want.

Sounds like your cousin means a lot to you.

I have *no idea* what I'm going to say to him. It's been so long.

What if he won't help me?

You're *family.* And *family* will *always* help one another. No matter *what.*

Gotta *trust* that.

Yeah.

I'm going to get you some *waffles.* You get some *food* in your stomach and then you go find this cousin of yours. It'll work out just *fine.*

Where did everybody--

Fire's not much good if the *oxygen* runs away.

Hello, Jennifer.

BONE, IDAHO.

WANDA!

I thought I could talk to her. I didn't want to fight.

But she's **stronger** than normal, Cap. She's **very, very** strong.

You are NOTHING to She-Hulk!

GO HIDE! Hide like Jennifer!

BOOOMMM!!

This isn't good, Cap. I don't know what it is, but her **strength** levels are nearing the **Hulk's**.

We need to lead her **out** of town, Cap.

Away from these people.

She's **afraid**. And **fear** is what **triggers** the **transformation**.

RAAAYY!

Fortunately, *Iron Man* heard me out. Even recommended me to the *Avengers*.

Maybe you'd prefer a *sonic* arrow?

It's where I made my *mark* in this world.

Where I met a lot of very *good* friends.

Which is why, when I heard Jennifer abandoned the team-- like I did a few times myself--

SHE-HULK KNOCK YOU DOWN!

I just didn't think *helping* would involve pulling out the *big toys.*

How about the "you-shouldn't-have-cheesed-off-Clint-Barton-today" arrow?

Even though I'm prone to arguments-- I *do* hate fighting with *friends.*

--I headed out here to help.

In Jen's case, though--I guess this is more like foreplay.

--Bruce Banner.

Bannerrr?

Unn...Banner? What are you doing--

In the area, *wandering* as always.

Rrn.

Cracked rib.

Do yourself a favor, Hawkeye. Stay *quiet*. Don't *move*.

Avengers business. *Not* yours.

I helped *found* the Avengers, mister.

And *I'll* talk her *down*.

It's *all* my fault.

When I gave you that *blood transfusion*, I passed on my *disease*.

I infected you--

No.

Bruce made *Jennifer* better.

Made *fear* go away.

She-Hulk loves Bruce.

STUPID HUMANS SHOULD LEAVE HULKS ALONE!

RRRRARARAR!

FSSSHHTT

I've changed the surrounding *ice* and *snow* into *steam*.

It should *confuse* them for a moment. I...nnnn...

What is it?

Think my *wrist* is broken. But I can *handle* the pain...

I've got to keep them *away* from one another. Jennifer's *strong*--but no match for the Hulk.

So we just play *tag* with the *green guys* until--

Until more *help* arrives. Keep them from *killing* each other or going back to *town* to face *Uncle Sam.*

AVENGERS.

All right.

Let's take a peek--

--inside.

It's a **three** movement mechanical system.

Meaning I need to **fool** the three clocks into thinking fourteen hours in **total** have passed--

--so I can enter the **code** and unlock the standard mechanism.

Locking rod leads to--

--the **clocks**.

Trick is, we've got to **attack** all three timers at once. Change them all at the **same time**.

Which is why I brought some help.

You guys ready?

Jack?

I *swear* I didn't mean to *do* this, Cap. I--

I *know*, Jack. We ALL know.

You think you can *pull* this off? Do a *limited* detonation and then retain the fallout?

I was only in the *Zero Room* a few hours. I can feel my suit *burning* apart already. Close to...*blacking* out.

If I *let loose* like this-- even if I *can* contain it-- I'm not sure I'll be able to *reabsorb* it. I could turn this place into a *desert*.

I could *kill* Jennifer.

Maybe... maybe I should just *fly* away from here. Just get away.

Jack, it'--*zzz*-- Iron Man.

I know these last few months have been *hard*. These last --*kzzz*-- *years* even.

I met you when you were just getting into the *game* and whether you *know* it or *not*, you've-- *zzzz*--a *very* long way. It's time to take another b--*kzzzt*--step.

It's time to *trust* yourself.

You-- *zzzz*--me?

Jack?

Is he there? Is he--

I *hear* you. Get everyone clear, Mr. Stark.

I'm going in.

Roger that. Good luck, kid.

Hulk sm--

Bombs away.

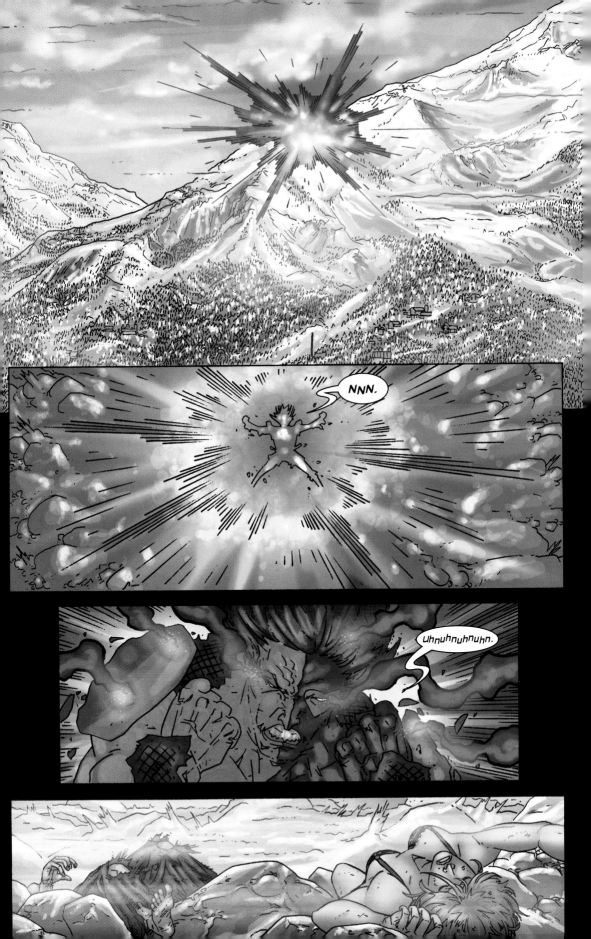

Jennifer...

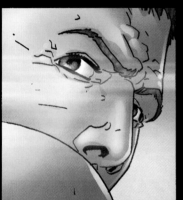

You're better off with *them*. And I'm better off...

Bruce?

She-Hulk.

Welcome back.

Can't believe he pulled it off.

Is he going to be all right?

I'm not sure, Jennifer. Jack's never *exhausted* his *supply* of energy and then *restored* it. The best we can do now is get him back to the *Zero Room*.

Vegetation on that *mountainside* probably won't regrow for *years*...

Watch it, Jen. *Don't* get too *close*. Hate to have the *cycle* start all *over* again.

How do you think Jack returned me to--

He can see *radiation* like we can see *colors*. The last time he *touched* you, he may have been able to *re-charge* your body with the proper dose of *gamma radiation*.

It probably took the remaining bit of *willpower* he had left.

We just can't *risk* having you two come in contact with one another again.

How are we going to make sure we *don't*?

One of you is going to have to leave the team.

Hey, Hawkeye!

This is for helping me.

And this is for shooting my *cousin* with an *arrow*.

You know, I really *missed* her.

Well then, Clint.

Does this mean you're *back*?

Yeah.

I'm back.

I did all that, didn't I? Lord, I never meant to--

How many--

Wounded? The count's at *seventy-two.*

No deaths.

Iron Man already has *Stark Enterprises* on the way. They'll rebuild this town, but...

...it's going to take time. And many of the *wounds* here... they'll never *heal.*

The *media* is blaming the *Hulk.*

But--

Let them say what they want.

I see them.

Give me the magnifying glass!

HEY! KNOCK IT OFF!

...'fore we squash *you* too.

Leave 'em alone, Danny.

Cassie Lang. The Insect-Girl.

Get outta here, Insect-Girl...

I wouldn't do that if I were you.

Why *not*?

Because the ants won't like it.

AHAHAHA!

They won't like it and they're smarter than you think. You know how fast fire ants could do it?

What?

Do *what*, Insect-Girl?

How fast they could swarm over you while you're sleeping. Crawl into your mouth...

Do you know how *fast* they could *eat* you from the *inside out*?

'Cause if you hurt them--that's what they'll do.

She's... she's lying, right?

C'mon, Lance.

You're a total *freak*, Lang.

I'd rather be a freak than a stupid *boy*.

Excuse me.

00:34:01

Avengers Embassy.
Sub-basement.
The Zero-Room.

00:34:00

00:33:59

It's never going to get *easier*, Jack.

Isn't that what *Dad* used to tell you? You have to know when to *bluff*--

"-- and when to fold."

Forgive me for being *out* of the *loop* but let's look at the situation again.

Jack of Hearts absorbs radiation. That's his thing. Has to spend *fourteen hours* a day locked in that Vault.

The Zero Room.

And Jack's been slowly *stealing* the *gamma radiation* from She-Hulk, right?

If he touches her--he *triggers* her change back to human form. Or maybe makes her *Hulk-out* Banner-style again.

He's not doing it on *purpose,* Clint.

Someone just needs to make the *call.*

ARRRAA!

Nnnrraa.

No more. You're coming *with* me.

Jack, you...you can't take him anywhere. *You* have to get back--

I finally see it now. You're *right*, Scott. It's not about bettering *myself*, *is* it?

It's not about being *asked* for help or being looked *up* to. It's just about improving the *world*. Making it a *safe* place for this and the next generation.

What are you doing?

He...hurt his own *daughter*. I don't know *why* or *how*, but he *did*.

I'm an Avenger.

So I'm avenging.

Take care of your family, Scott.

BWOOOSHH!

JACK!! WAIT!

Trust men, and they will
be true to you; treat them
greatly, and they will
show themselves great.
--Ralph Waldo Emerson

NEXT: LIONHEART OF AVALON